First Wave
Subject 117

Written by
CHRIS BRANCATO

Level 2

Retold by Karen Holmes
Series Editors: Andy Hopkins and Jocelyn Potter

Pearson Education Limited
Edinburgh Gate, Harlow,
Essex CM20 2JE, England
and Associated Companies throughout the world.

ISBN 0 582 43055 0

First published 2000

Produced under licence from Pearson Television International Limited

Typeset by Ferdinand Pageworks, London
Set in 11/14pt Bembo
Printed in Spain by Mateu Cromo, S. A. Pinto (Madrid)

Published by Pearson Education Limited in association with
Penguin Books Ltd, both companies being subsidiaries of Pearson Plc

For a complete list of the titles available in the Penguin Readers series please write to your local
Pearson Education office or to: Marketing Department, Penguin Longman Publishing,
5 Bentinck Street, London W1M 5RN.

Contents

Introduction

Then something happened, something strange and ugly. I saw something move in Hannah's neck . . .

Strange tentacles came out of her arms and legs. Long, thin, green tentacles. They moved around my neck and across my face. They were wet and cold.

"I can't see," I cried.

The tentacles closed over my eyes and mouth. I started to fight them, but they were too strong.

"Hannah!" I shouted. "Hannah, help me!"

Cade Foster has a good job and a beautiful wife. Suddenly things start to go wrong. He loses his job and his money. He sees strange things, pictures in his head. Is he going crazy? Or does somebody—or something—want to hurt him?

First Wave is an exciting story for television, and the story begins with *Subject 117*. Chris Brancato, the writer, also worked on the *X-Files* and *The Outer Limits*.

Francis Ford Coppola made *Subject 117* for television. His most famous movies are *The Godfather* and *Apocalypse Now*.

My name is Cade Foster.

Chapter 1   My Name is Cade Foster

Aliens will come to Earth three times.
The first time, nobody will know them. They will be men
and women.
The second time, the aliens will kill nineteen million
people.
The third time, the aliens will destroy the Earth.
On the seventh day, a man will walk on Earth. Only he
can stop the aliens . . .

From *The Book of Nostradamus*

My name is Cade Foster. For many years I was a thief. I took
money from banks and stores, and the police were very interested
in me.

Then I met my wife, Hannah, and my life changed. I loved her
very much and I wanted her to be happy. She didn't want to
marry a thief, so I found a job. I started working for Viceroy, a big
company. Viceroy sells strong locks to other companies.

Life was good. But last summer I started to see strange things.
Bad things. Nobody saw them—only me. There were pictures
inside my head. Sometimes I saw a man, a stranger. I saw his face
for a minute and then it went away. And sometimes I heard a
voice in my head. It said, "Nineteen."

I was afraid . . .

◆

I was in Mr. Dray's office. He was the boss of another large
company.

"You want good locks in your offices," I told him. "We're
living in a bad world."

"I *have* good locks, Mr. Foster. They're Goodwin locks. I only bought them last month, and they cost eighty thousand dollars."

I looked around me.

"Your locks aren't bad," I said. "But . . ."

I walked across the room. There was a box in the wall behind a picture. I broke the lock and opened the box very quickly.

". . . but they aren't very good. Viceroy locks are better."

"OK," Mr. Dray said. He looked unhappily at the open box. "Show me."

I opened my bag and took out—a head. A man's head. There was blood on the head and blood on my hands.

The head spoke to me. "Nineteen," it said.

"I—"

"What is it?" Mr. Dray asked.

I looked again. There was nothing in my hands, only the lock.

"Nothing," I said. "It's my stomach . . . I had lunch in the company restaurant. Now, here's a really good lock. Look at this."

◆

Later that day, I met my wife and some friends in a restaurant. It was a hot, sunny afternoon, so we sat outside.

"I don't understand," I said. "I see things, strange things. They aren't really there. The first time, I was in the park. Then another time I was in the car. Today it happened in Mr. Dray's office. I opened my bag and I saw . . ."

"What did you see?" my friend laughed.

"A head," I said. "A man's head. It had a mustache and brown hair. It was only his head and there was a lot of blood."

"Who was he?"

"I don't know," I said.

"You're crazy," my friend said. "What did Mr. Dray think?"

"Oh, he was fine. I didn't tell him about the head. I sold him the locks."

I opened my bag and took out—a head.

"Excuse me," Hannah said. She left the table and walked away. I followed her, but a waiter stopped me.

"I'm sorry, sir. There's a problem with your American Express card."

"My card's fine. Can you try again?"

"No, sir," the waiter said. "The company says that we have to destroy it."

"What? Listen, I have to talk to my wife. I'll be back in a minute."

I ran after Hannah. She wasn't happy.

"What's happening to you?" she asked. "You can laugh about these stories with our friends, but they really aren't funny."

"I'm sorry, Hannah," I said.

"Something's wrong with you. I talked to Mary. Her uncle's a doctor at Northwestern Hospital."

"I talked to five different doctors. You know that. They say I'm all right."

"Mary's uncle says there's somebody at a different hospital. He can help you."

"Hannah, I'm busy. I have to work. I have a job. Remember?"

"Then take a vacation," Hannah said angrily.

"But it doesn't happen very often."

"Cade, I'm afraid for you."

"Don't be afraid! I'm fine. Let's walk."

"And leave our friends?"

"They're OK."

We walked through the yard of the restaurant. Hannah was very beautiful in her long blue dress. Her hair fell down her back.

"I love you," I said. "And I have something for you."

I gave her a locket. Inside, there was a photo of her and me and the words: *Always, Cade.*

"It's beautiful," she said. "Thank you."

She put the locket around her neck.

4

"Do you remember that picture?" I asked. "It was a really cold day."

"You put your arms around me and I was warm."

"You're my best friend, Hannah," I said. "Things are difficult now but they were hard before. We were OK then and we'll be OK now, too."

♦

That night, in bed, Hannah said, "I love you, too."

I took her in my arms but something was wrong. I looked up. At the bottom of the bed I saw him again—the man with the mustache and the brown hair.

"What's wrong?" Hannah asked.

"Nothing," I said. "It's nothing."

Chapter 2   "Who wants to hurt me?"

The next day my boss, Mr. Birmingham, called me into his office. He was angry and unhappy.

"Sit down, Cade," he said. "I want to talk to you."

I sat down in a chair near his desk.

"Somebody sent these papers to me," Birmingham said. He had a lot of papers in his hand. I could see the words at the top of the first paper: *From the office of the Chicago Police.*

Mr. Birmingham started to read.

"'Cade Foster is a thief. He is the best thief in the state. He is very smart and very dangerous. The police in thirty-seven cities in the United States of America are interested in this man.'"

"That happened when I was younger. I'm not a thief now," I told him. "I stopped. I met Hannah and I got a job. Who sent those papers to you?"

"I can't tell you," Birmingham said. "But you can't work here.

I'm sorry, Cade. I like you, and your work's very good. But I don't want a thief in my company. We sell locks! Our customers won't buy locks from thieves."

"Who sent those papers?" I asked again. "You have to tell me."

"Leave this office or I'll call the police," Birmingham said.

I left the room.

◆

I wanted some money, so I went to the bank.

"I want to take out three hundred dollars, please," I said to the girl in the bank.

She went to her computer. A minute later, she came back again.

"I'm sorry, sir. I can't give you any money. I looked at the names of our customers on the computer. There's no Cade Foster."

"But that's crazy!" I said. "This is my bank. My money's here."

"We don't have any of your money in this bank, sir," the girl said. "Please leave."

"I have more than five thousand dollars in this bank," I said angrily.

"Leave the bank now, or I'll call the police," the girl said.

I ran out of the bank.

For the next three hours, I walked through the city streets. I was angry and afraid.

"Who sent those papers to Birmingham?" I thought. "Where's my money? Yesterday it was in the bank and now it's not there. What's happening to me? Who wants to hurt me?"

◆

It was dark when I got home. The front door was open and the window was open, too. There was food on the floor in the kitchen.

"Was there a fight here?" I thought. I walked into the sitting-room. "Somebody broke the tables and chairs. Look at this glass! What happened? And where's Hannah?"

"Who sent those papers?" I asked again. "You have to tell me."

Then I saw the number nineteen on the walls. There were big red numbers on every wall.

"Hannah!" I shouted. "Hannah! Where are you?"

I looked in every room downstairs, but I couldn't find her.

"Hannah!" I shouted again.

I ran up the stairs and looked in the bedroom. No Hannah. Then I kicked open the bathroom door and I saw her. She was on the floor.

"Hannah, it's me—Cade. It's OK."

"I heard noises," she cried. "I was afraid, so I came in here. Who was in our house?"

"I don't know," I said. "But I'm going to find him."

I put my arms around her.

◆

Later that night, I went back to Viceroy, to Mr. Birmingham's office. Quietly, I opened the door of his room. I looked at the strong lock on his desk.

"No problem," I thought. I opened the lock with a special knife.

I opened the desk and found the papers, the papers about me. There was a name on one of them—Detective Samuel Hitchens, Chicago Police.

I didn't know Samuel Hitchens. Who was he? Why did he send those papers to Mr. Birmingham? I wanted to find this man.

I wrote down Hitchens's address, then I put the papers back in Mr. Birmingham's desk. I turned off the light and quietly left the office.

◆

When I arrived home, Hannah was very angry.

"It's late. Where were you?" she asked. Then she saw the knife in my hand.

"You used that knife before, when you were a thief. Cade,

I opened the desk and found the papers, the papers about me.

what are you doing? Were you in somebody's house? A bank? Did you take anything? You told me—"

"I went to Mr. Birmingham's office," I said. "Something happened today, Hannah. A policeman—Samuel Hitchens—sent my papers to my boss at Viceroy. I don't know this man, but he wanted me to lose my job. And he won, because I lost it this morning!"

"Oh, no! Cade—what are we going to do?"

"Then there's the money," I said. "Yesterday my American Express card didn't work at the restaurant. Remember? This afternoon I went to the bank—and we don't have any money. The bank didn't know me. What's happening to us?"

"Who wants to hurt us?" Hannah asked.

"I don't know," I said. "But I think Samuel Hitchens knows. I've got his home address, and I'm going to see him tomorrow."

Chapter 3   "No! Sam!"

The next morning, I drove to Samuel Hitchens's house. There was a car in the street outside the house. A man with dark hair sat inside the car. There was a woman next to him. She had light brown hair and wore a black jacket.

"Who are they? Are they watching Hitchens's house? Or are they waiting for me?" I thought. "Do I know them?"

A woman opened the door of the house. She was about forty-five years old and she had a pretty face. She took my hand and pulled me inside.

"Please help me!" she said.

"I'm looking for Samuel Hitchens," I told her.

"I called 911."

"Why? What happened?"

"My husband's in the bathroom—and he's got a gun. Please! Help me!"

I followed her up the stairs.

"He's afraid," the woman said. "Something's happening to him. He sees things, strange things. I don't see them, but they're making him crazy."

We stood outside the bathroom door.

"Please come out, Sam," Mrs. Hitchens said.

"Go away!" he cried.

"Somebody wants to hurt him," Mrs. Hitchens said to me.

"Who?"

"I don't know. Sam lost his job with the police. Our American Express cards don't work. And the bank says we don't have any money."

"That's happened to me, too," I said.

Mrs. Hitchens pushed the bathroom door again.

"Sam, please open the door. Somebody wants to talk to you."

"Is there somebody in our house?" Sam asked.

"He's a nice man. He—"

We heard the noise of a gun.

"No! Sam!" Mrs. Hitchens cried.

I kicked open the door. Hitchens was dead. He was face down on the floor and the gun was next to him.

I turned him over. I knew his face, his mustache, his brown hair. I heard his voice inside my head: "Nineteen ..."

Mrs. Hitchens stayed with her husband. I couldn't help her.

Quickly I went into Hitchens's bedroom. There were a lot of old newspapers on a large desk near the window. Every newspaper had a story about the same person: Mayhew, now in Wilsonville Special Hospital.

"Mayhew—I know that name," I thought. "He's a dangerous

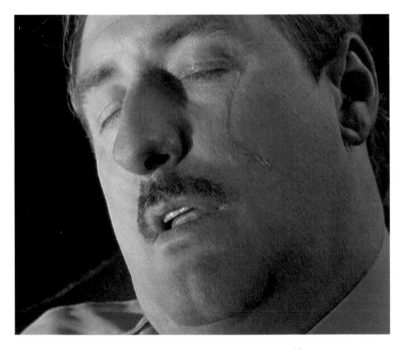

Hitchens was dead.

man. He killed his wife and children, and the police put him in a special hospital. Why are these papers on Hitchens's desk?"

Next to the newspapers, I saw Hitchens's police badge.

"Maybe I can use this," I thought, and I took it.

Mrs. Hitchens was in the bathroom with her husband. I heard the sound of police cars. Quietly, I left the house and drove to Wilsonville Special Hospital.

Chapter 4   "You're an alien!"

The hospital was outside town. It was a big old house with a high wall around the yard.

A woman in a white dress opened the door.

"Can I help you?" she asked.

"I want to speak to a doctor," I said. "It's about Mayhew. It's very important."

"I'll get him," the woman said.

A young doctor came out, and I showed him the police badge.

"My name's Detective Hitchens," I told him. "I'm from the Chicago Police. I want to see Mayhew. I have to ask him some questions."

"Come inside," the doctor said. "You can talk to Mayhew, but be careful. He's dangerous. Last week he almost killed somebody. He's in this room." The doctor unlocked a door.

I went into the room, and the doctor waited outside. Mayhew sat in a chair in the middle of the room. He was about fifty years old. He had long hair, and he wore dirty old blue jeans and a green shirt. His eyes were cold and angry—I was afraid of his eyes. There was a rope around his hands.

"I can't move," he said. "They say I'm crazy."

"Are you?" I asked.

"Yes, I'm crazy." He laughed. It was an ugly sound. "You're not a detective."

"No, I'm not. But I saw pictures in my head, pictures of a stranger. I know now that his name's Detective Samuel Hitchens. But he's dead. I found your name in some newspapers in his house."

"I see things, too," Mayhew said. "Somebody wanted to hurt me, so they took my money—thirty-seven million dollars. I paid seventy-five men, and they looked for the money for me. But they found nothing."

"You killed your family," I said. "Why? Did you hate them?"

"No!" Mayhew cried. "I loved my wife and my children. But they got them, they got my family."

"Who? Who are *they*?" I asked.

"They're aliens!" Mayhew said. "They were in my house. They followed me everywhere, and they watched me. They knew everything about me. There were cameras in the house. The aliens are watching you, too. Did you know that? There are cameras in *your* house. And then I knew—my wife and children! The aliens were inside them. They wanted to kill me—so I killed them!"

"This man *is* crazy," I thought. "But I see things too. And the bank lost my money. Maybe . . ."

"Find the book," Mayhew said. "I wrote everything in a book. It's in the middle of my backyard, under the red eye. Read the book, and then you'll understand."

He looked at me again. Suddenly he was angry.

"Who are you?" he shouted. "Why are you here? Who sent you?"

"I want to help you," I said.

"You're not a detective! You're an alien! You're an alien!" He pulled at the rope on his hands. He wanted to hurt me.

The doctor came into the room.

"Find the book," Mayhew said.

"Please leave," he said to me. "He can't answer anymore questions."

There was another man outside the door, a man with dark hair. Did I know his face?

"*Do* I know him?" I thought. I wanted to speak to him, but the man walked quickly away.

◆

I went home and told Hannah about Mayhew. "We're going to Mayhew's house," I said. "I want to find this book. But first . . ."

I started to look around the house. I took our clothes out of the closet and the books from the shelves. I ran from room to room.

"What are you doing?" Hannah asked.

"Mayhew says they're watching us. There are cameras here, in the house."

"Cade, I want you to see the doctor. We can go to that other hospital next week. Please, tell me you'll go. It's important."

"We don't have any money," I said angrily. "Remember?"

"My mom will give us the money."

I turned and looked at her.

"Your mom knows about this? Hannah!" I cried. "Why did you tell her?"

"I'm afraid, Cade," my wife said. "You're so strange these days. The doctor—"

"A doctor can't help me. Something or somebody wants to hurt me. They hurt Mayhew and Hitchens—now they're going to hurt me."

"Mayhew is crazy," Hannah cried.

"But he saw things, things inside his head. And he lost his money—"

"Mayhew killed his family! You listened to him? He's a crazy man. See the doctor, Cade, or I'll leave this house. I'll leave you."

She ran out of the house into the yard. I looked for the camera in every room. I went into the bathroom.

"Hannah!" I shouted. "Come here!"

She came back into the house. "What is it now?"

"This shower always drips," I said.

"What?"

"The shower drips. Drip, drip, drip. Remember? And now it isn't dripping."

"What are you talking about, Cade?"

I pulled the shower from the wall. There it was, inside the shower head. A very, very small camera.

"Somebody put this in the shower," I said. "Mayhew was right. They *are* watching us. They can see and hear everything in this house."

"You have to tell the police," Hannah said.

"The police can't help me. Something's happening, Hannah. There are cameras in our house. Hitchens, Mayhew, me—we all saw bad things. Now Hitchens is dead and Mayhew is crazy. What will happen to *me*?"

Chapter 5 "Who *are* these aliens?"

Hannah came with me to Mayhew's house. Mayhew was a rich man and he had a big old house with a large backyard.

"This is a big yard. Where do we start?" Hannah said.

"Mayhew says the book is in the middle of the yard, under the red eye," I said.

"What's the red eye?" Hannah asked.

Hannah came with me to Mayhew's house.

We walked through the yard and looked at the flowers and the fruit trees. Then I saw something. At the foot of a tall tree, the ground was different.

"Let's try here," I said.

We pulled away the flowers and we found it. Under the ground there was a box, an old black box with some red glass on top.

"Cade!" Hannah said. "It's the red eye."

Quickly we pulled the box out of the ground, and I broke the lock. Inside we found a book. Hannah looked at the name on the first page.

"Nostradamus?" Hannah said. "I know the name. Who was he?"

"He was a doctor. He lived in France and he died in 1566. He could see into the future. Some people read his books now. They think the world will end this year. Look at this page."

We read the words: *On the seventh day, a man will walk on Earth. Only he can stop the aliens.*

"I'm afraid," Hannah said. "I don't like this place. Let's get out of here."

"I want to see Mayhew again. What do these words mean? Who *are* these aliens? Maybe he can tell me."

"No!" Hannah said. "Go to the police!"

"Please, Hannah. I'm going back to Wilsonville Special Hospital."

"OK," she said. "But I'm coming with you."

◆

We drove quickly to the hospital. The young doctor met me at the door.

"You're Detective Hitchens," the doctor said. "You saw Mayhew yesterday. I'm sorry, but you can't see him again. He died this morning."

"What happened to him?" I asked.

"I want to see Mayhew again. What do these words mean?"

"He used the rope around his hands. He was crazy. It often happens."

"Why?" I thought. "Why is Mayhew dead now, the day after my visit?"

"Can I look in his room?" I asked.

The doctor opened the door.

"Stay here," I said to Hannah.

"OK, detective," she said. She smiled at me.

I went into the room.

◆

Outside the door, Hannah waited for me. She saw a man and a woman. The man was tall and thin, with dark hair. The woman had light brown hair and she wore a black jacket. They came to her. Carefully, the man took Hannah's arm and they walked away . . .

◆

"Why did you die, Mayhew?" I thought. "Did you leave a note for me?"

I looked around and felt the white walls and the floor with my hands.

"There's nothing here," I thought. I looked at the chair. "Mayhew sat there. He couldn't move . . ."

And then I found it—a small paper inside the arm of Mayhew's chair. There was an address on it—19 Haven Street.

"Nineteen—it's always nineteen," I thought. "Why is that number important?"

I left the room and found Hannah.

"Look at this, Hannah!" I said. "The number nineteen is in my head. Sometimes I hear a voice saying 'nineteen.' It was on the walls of our house. Now I have this address from Mayhew—19 Haven Street. I want to go there."

"You can go, but I'm not going with you," Hannah said angrily.

19

"This is crazy! I want you to call the police, and I want you to see a doctor. Call them now, or I'll leave you! I really will leave you."

"OK, I'll call the police," I said.

"And I don't want to go home," Hannah said. "I don't want to be near those cameras. I hate our house now. I'm afraid there."

"We'll go to a hotel. Let's go."

Chapter 6   "Hannah, help me!"

We stopped at a small hotel near the town. It was a cheap place and the rooms were small and ugly.

"This isn't very nice," Hannah said.

"We can't go to a better hotel. My American Express card doesn't work and we have no money."

I tried to call the police, but it was very late.

"You want to speak to a detective?" the policeman said. "There's nobody here. Call tomorrow."

"OK, I'll come to the police station tomorrow morning," I said. I put the phone down.

"Why didn't you tell that policeman about it?" Hannah asked.

"He's not going to listen to me. What can I say? 'Sir, there are aliens here on Earth'? Mayhew was crazy. The police will think I'm crazy too."

"So what are we going to do?"

"Tomorrow, I'll go to the police and I'll call the FBI," I said. "Maybe they can help us. I'll tell them about Mayhew and this address in Haven Street."

"Good," Hannah said.

"And tomorrow I want you to go to Seattle. Stay with your mom and dad for a week."

"I'm not going to Seattle without you," Hannah said angrily.

"Hannah, you *are* going," I said. "I lost my job and my money. I don't want to lose you. Tomorrow you're going to Seattle. Please."

"OK," Hannah said.

I looked at her. There was something wrong. Her eyes were different—cold and dead.

"What's wrong?" she asked. "You're looking at me very strangely."

"Nothing's wrong," I said. "It's nothing. Everything will be all right. Let's go to bed and sleep."

I went into the bathroom. When I came out, Hannah was in bed. I got in next to her and put my arms around her.

Then something happened, something strange and ugly. I saw something move in Hannah's neck, then something moved inside her arms, too. Her face changed. This was not my Hannah!

Strange tentacles came out of her arms and legs. Long, thin, green tentacles. They moved around my neck and across my face. They were wet and cold.

Long, thin, green tentacles. They moved around my neck.

"I can't see," I cried.

The tentacles closed over my eyes and mouth. I started to fight them, but they were too strong.

"Hannah!" I shouted. "Hannah, help me!"

She didn't speak. Her eyes were closed.

Hannah's locket was around her neck and I caught it in my hand. Then I fell to the floor. Everything was dark . . .

♦

Slowly the tentacles moved back inside Hannah's arms and legs. Hannah stood up and looked down at me. She didn't try to help me.

She didn't put on her clothes. She walked out of the room, and out of the hotel. Nobody saw her.

There was a black car outside the hotel, and Hannah climbed inside it. The driver was a man with dark hair. Next to him was a woman with light brown hair. She wore a black jacket. They got out and opened the back door.

They took something heavy out of the back of the car. It was another woman, another Hannah. Her eyes were closed and she didn't move. They carried her up the stairs and into the hotel . . .

Chapter 7 "Nobody can help me now"

When I woke up, I was on the floor.

"What happened?" I thought. "Why am I here on the floor?"

I opened my eyes. Hannah's locket was in my hand. I looked around the room. Then I saw Hannah next to the bed. She didn't move. Was she dead?

"No!" I said. "Please, Hannah, wake up!"

I looked at her. There was a locket around her neck. But there was a locket in my hand, too. I opened the locket in my hand. There was nothing inside it.

There was the photo of her and me and the words: Always, Cade.

I moved to Hannah and opened the locket around her neck. There was the photo of her and me and the words: *Always, Cade.*

I took her in my arms. This was Hannah, my beautiful wife. And she was dead.

"No, Hannah!" I cried. "No!"

She didn't move.

"Please get up, Hannah," I said. "Open your eyes and talk to me. I love you, you know that. You can't leave me now. Everything will be OK. Please open your eyes, and I'll get us out of here."

I heard the noise of police cars. The noise got louder and louder. Suddenly somebody kicked the door open. It was a policeman.

"Sir, move away!" the policeman said. There was a gun in his hand. A second policeman stood behind him.

"Stay away from me," I said.

"Move away from the woman, sir," the policeman said. "Move very slowly."

I put Hannah back onto the floor. The policeman put the gun to my head.

"Let's go," he said. "Put on your clothes. You're coming with us." He threw my shirt at me.

The second policeman went to Hannah and looked at her carefully.

"She's dead," he said. "What happened here?"

Why were the police here? Who called them? Who saw Hannah and me in the hotel? We didn't see anybody when we came in.

I heard Mayhew's words again: "They're watching you . . ."

"We have to take you to the police station," the first policeman said.

He put his hand on my arm. I kicked at him with my foot and hit him on the leg. His gun fell from his hand to the floor. Then the second policeman tried to hit me, but I kicked him, too. I kicked him again and again.

The two men were on the floor. They didn't move. Suddenly the room was very quiet.

I put on my shirt and pants.

"I have to get out of here," I thought. I looked back at Hannah, but I couldn't help her now.

I ran out of the room. My car was outside and I jumped in. I started it and drove away.

"Nobody can help me now," I thought. "There are aliens in the police, and maybe in the FBI, too. I can't go to them. But I *can* go to 19 Haven Street . . ."

Chapter 8   "Nineteen—always nineteen"

Nineteen Haven Street was an old house near the river. It was dirty and there was no glass in the windows. Nobody lived there. There was a big number nineteen above the door.

"Nineteen—always nineteen," I thought.

The door was open. I took my flashlight from the car and slowly walked inside.

It was very dark and cold. I went into the first room and shined my flashlight across the floor and walls. There were some old chairs, a table, and another door.

I went slowly through the door into the second room. Was anybody there? I shined the flashlight in front of me and saw—nothing.

There were some stairs at the end of the room. I ran carefully up them. At the top there was another door, and I opened it.

I was in a large, square room. It was full of white light, so I turned off the flashlight. There was nothing on the floor of the room, but on every wall there were big photos. There were hundreds of large photos of men and women. Under each picture there was the word "subject" and then a number.

I walked around the room and looked at each photo. There were men and women, young and old. I didn't know them—they were strangers to me.

Then I saw two pictures on one of the walls.

"*You're* not strangers," I thought. "I know you."

The first picture was a photo of Mayhew. Under the photo were the words: *Subject 110—dead.* The second picture was a photo of Hitchens with the words: *Subject 114—dead.*

I looked at two or three other pictures, and then I saw it.

I saw a picture of a young man with short, dark hair. He had brown eyes and a friendly smile. I knew that face well because it

I went into the first room and shined my flashlight across the floor and walls.

Under the photo were the words: Subject 117—he will die today.

was my face. Under the photo were the words: *Subject 117—he will die today.*

Who put these photos in this room? Why were they here? Who were these people? And why was I "Subject 117"?

I wanted those photos.

"Now the police will have to listen to me," I thought. "Something very bad is happening. Hitchens and Mayhew are dead—and I'm going to die, too!"

I pulled the three photos from the wall. Then I heard a noise.

I looked out the window. Outside the building, there were two police cars. The police—again! Here at 19 Haven Street. How did they know? They always knew.

"Don't move!" a policeman shouted. "Put the flashlight down. Do it now!"

"Help me!" I cried, "Come inside the house and look. Then you'll understand."

"Don't speak," the policeman said. He had a gun in his hand.

"Look at the pictures!" I said. "Look at these pictures!"

I ran down the stairs and gave them to him. The policeman took the pictures and looked at them.

"What are these?" he asked. "I can't see anything."

"Can't you see?" I cried. "Mayhew, Hitchens—me. In the photos. Look at them!"

But there were no photos in his hand—the paper was white.

"Put your hands behind your back," the policeman said. "We're taking you to the police station."

"No!" I shouted. "They were there—photos of me, Mayhew, and Hitchens! I'm Subject 117! You have to listen to me! Please listen to me!"

"Get in," the policeman said. He pushed me into his police car.

"No!" I cried. And then I understood. Why did the police come to 19 Haven Street? Because they knew. And how did they know? Because they knew everything about me.

I started to shout and fight, but the policemen were very strong. I couldn't get out of the car.

"You're an alien!" I cried to the man next to me. "You're all aliens!"

Chapter 9 "This is Subject 117"

The next day, I stood in front of a police detective.

"Please! Listen to me," I cried. "I didn't hurt Hannah. Something's happening to me—"

"Be quiet!" the man said.

"But you don't understand. There are people—things—out there. They killed Hannah and they want to kill me—"

The detective didn't listen to me.

"You're a dangerous man, Mr. Foster," he said. "You killed a young and beautiful woman. She was your wife, and you killed her. I'm sending you to Wilsonville Special Hospital. You're going to stay there."

He turned to another policeman.

"Take him away," he said.

The police put me in a car. I saw a woman across the street. I didn't know her but I watched her carefully. There was something strange about her.

She put her hand up to her mouth, and I saw something red on her finger. Red glass. The red eye. I remembered the red glass

She put her hand up to her mouth, and I saw something red on her finger.

on the box in Mayhew's yard. Was she an alien? Or was she a friend?

The car started to move.

"Wilsonville Special Hospital," one of the policemen said. "That's a bad place, a place for crazy people. You'll be there for a long, long time."

♦

After twenty minutes, we arrived at the hospital. The same young doctor came to the door.

"Detective Hitchens?" he asked. "Or is it Cade Foster?" He looked at the policemen. "Take him inside."

The policemen put me in a small white room. There was only one chair in the room. They put rope around my hands so I couldn't move.

The policemen left the room and the doctor came back in. There were two other men with him. One was tall and thin with black hair. The other was smaller and his hair was gray. I knew the man with the dark hair.

"I saw you," I thought. "I saw you in a car outside Sam Hitchens's house. I saw you here, too, on my first visit to the hospital."

The doctor had some pills in his hand. He stood over me.

"Open wide," he said. He pushed the pills into my mouth.

The three men stood and watched me. After two minutes, I closed my eyes.

"He's asleep now, so we can talk," the doctor said to the other men. "This is Subject 117. There are 117 types of people on Earth. This man is type 117. And he's different from the other men.

"When we gave pills to the other men, they saw strange pictures in their head. They also lost their jobs and their money. They went crazy very quickly and then we killed them."

"Subject 110 and Subject 114—they're dead now," the man with the dark hair said.

"Yes," said the doctor. "We gave the same pills to Subject 117. He didn't know, of course. He didn't see us. Then we took away Subject 117's job and his money. We were very smart. We took Hannah away, and we put an alien in her place. Now he thinks she's dead."

The other two men laughed.

"But Subject 117 is different," the doctor said. "When we hurt him, he fights us. He's not crazy. He visited Hitchens and Mayhew and he asked questions. He went to 19 Haven Street. Mayhew and Hitchens didn't find the place. Subject 117 is smart.

"Nothing stops Subject 117, so he's dangerous. But why is Subject 117 smarter than other men? Why is this man different? We want to know. We're going to cut open his head and look inside. We're going to learn everything about Subject 117. We have to learn everything about this type of man."

"This is very interesting," said the man with dark hair. "Good work, doctor."

"No," the doctor said. "Subject 117 did the work. He's a great fighter."

"Really?" the man said. "When we come to Earth again, we don't want to find dangerous men here. Are there more men of this type? What's his name?"

"They call him Cade Foster," the doctor said.

The man with gray hair moved near me and spoke. His voice was strange.

"Nineteen ... Nineteen ... The aliens will kill nineteen million people," he said.

"Now," the doctor said, "we'll leave Foster. Let's look at Subject 56. He was the boss of a large company. We only worked on him for two weeks and now he's crazy."

"Nineteen . . . Nineteen . . ."

"Only two weeks? That's very interesting," the man with dark hair said.

Chapter 10 "I know you're here . . ."

The three men left the room and closed the door. I opened my eyes. I wasn't really asleep—the pills were in my mouth, not in my stomach.

I pulled at the rope around my hands. It was strong, but I broke it with my teeth. Then I took the pills out of my mouth and put them on the chair. I made a number nineteen with the pills.

"The aliens like the number nineteen," I thought. "What did Nostradamus say? Nineteen million people will die. Somebody has to stop these aliens."

I looked at the lock on the door. It was a Goodwin lock. Quickly and quietly I opened the door and looked out.

There were a lot of people outside. I knew some of them. I saw Birmingham, my boss. Why was he here? And then I saw Mrs. Hitchens and the two policemen from the hotel. Why were they here, at Wilsonville Special Hospital?

I looked again at their cold, dead eyes.

"That's not Birmingham," I thought. "And that's not Mrs. Hitchens. These are aliens."

The doctor stopped Mrs. Hitchens.

"Good work," he said.

"Thank you," she said.

Mayhew was right! The aliens were here on Earth. Now I understood. I wasn't crazy. They weren't men and women—they were aliens. The doctor and the other men in the hospital, Mrs. Hitchens, my boss Birmingham, my beautiful Hannah—they were all aliens. My Hannah—they took her away and put an alien in her place.

"They want to watch the people on Earth," I thought. "They want to understand everything about us. That will make them strong. Then they'll come to Earth again and they'll destroy us."

I remembered Mayhew's book. Nostradamus said:

Aliens will come to Earth three times.
The first time, nobody will know them. They will be men and women.
The second time, the aliens will kill nineteen million people.
The third time, the aliens will destroy the Earth.
On the seventh day, a man will walk on Earth. Only he can stop the aliens . . .

"I know you're here . . ."

I moved quietly out of the room. A man tried to stop me, but I hit him. He fell to the floor. Other people came. They wanted to stop me, too, but I was too fast for them. I was angry and I was strong. Nobody could stop me now!

I ran quickly to get out of the hospital. There was a camera high up on the wall and I looked into it.

"Take my picture," I said angrily. "I want you to remember my face. I'm Subject 117. I know you're here. I know you're here. I know you're here . . ."

ACTIVITIES

Chapters 1–3

Before you read

1 Look at the pictures in this book. What do you think the story is about?

2 Find these words in your dictionary. They are all in the story. Use them in the sentences.

badge   blood   destroy   Earth   lock   locket

   a The policeman had a . . . . . on his hat.

   b He gave his wife a . . . . . for her birthday.

   c The fire will . . . . . the house!

   d I cut my hand and saw . . . . . on my finger.

   e The . . . . . moves around the sun.

   f She broke the . . . . . on the door.

3 Find the words in *italics* in your dictionary. Are the sentences right or wrong?

   a We only see *aliens* in movies.

   b A *million* dollars is more than a thousand dollars.

   c A *mustache* is hair on top of your head.

   d You wear a locket around your *neck*.

   e Your birthday is a *special* day.

   f A *thief* takes money from people.

   g You listen to people with your *voice*.

After you read

4 Answer the questions.

   a What is Cade Foster's job?

   b Why does Hannah want Cade to see a doctor?

   c What does Cade find on Hitchens's desk?

5 You are Cade Foster. You see strange pictures inside your head. Talk to another student about these pictures.

Chapters 4–6

Before you read

6 Who was Nostradamus? Why do people read his books?

7 Which sentences are right? Which sentences are wrong? Find the words in *italics* in your dictionary.

   a A shower can *drip*.

   b A river can *drip*.

   c *Rope* is strong. It does not break easily.

   d *Rope* is weak. It breaks easily.

   e Some animals in the ocean have *tentacles*.

   f Some people have *tentacles*.

After you read

8 Who says:

   a "Read the book, and then you'll understand."

   b "What's the red eye?"

   c "You're Detective Hitchens."

   d "Hannah, Help me!"

9 Work with another student.

   Student A: You are Cade Foster. You are at the hospital with Mayhew. Ask him questions.

   Student B: You are Mayhew. Tell Foster about the aliens.

Chapters 7–10

Before you read

10 You are Cade Foster. You wake up in the hotel room. What will you do next?

11 Read these sentences. What do you think the words in *italics* mean?

   a It was dark, so she turned on her *flashlight*.

   b He was sick, so the doctor gave him a *pill*.

   c The *subject* of the film was aliens.

   d A cat is a *type* of animal.

Now look in your dictionary. Were you right?

After you read

12 Why are these things important in the story?

    a the number nineteen   **b** the red eye

13 Why

    a does the detective send Cade Foster to the Wilsonville Special Hospital?

    b do the aliens want to study Cade Foster?

    c doesn't Cade Foster fall asleep?

    d is there a camera on the wall of the hospital?

14 You are Cade Foster. You run out of the Wilsonville Special Hospital. What will you do next? Tell other students.

Writing

15 You are Hannah Foster. You want your mom to send you some money. Write a letter to her. Tell her about Cade and his problems.

16 You are an alien. Write about the work of the doctors at the special hospital.

17 You are Cade Foster. You want somebody to know about the aliens. Write about them in a letter to a friend.

18 Write a story about aliens. Do they come to Earth? Are they friendly? What do they want to do? Start your story with the words: "It was almost midnight . . ."

Answers for the Activities in this book are published in our free resource packs for teachers, the Penguin Readers Factsheets, or available on a separate sheet. Please write to your local Pearson Education office or to: Marketing Department, Penguin Longman Publishing, 5 Bentinck Street, London W1M 5RN.